Brewed Between Worlds

TEA, COFFEE, AND THE ANGELS WHO DRINK THEM

MELODY R. GREEN

www.melodyrgreenauthor.com

Brewed Between Worlds
Tea, Coffee, and the Angels Who Drink Them
ISBN: 978-1-7641889-2-0 (paperback)
ISBN: 978-0-6457619-9-3 (ebook)
ASIN: BOGH8ZHDJQ

Cover Art by Jane Cornwell
www.janecornwell.co.uk
jane.cornwell.uk@gmail.com

Interior Book Design and Editing by Sarah Lemcke
www.allintheedit.com
sarah@allintheedit.com

For every soul who has ever found comfort in a warm cup,
magic in a quiet moment,
or hope in a story.
And for the angels—
who remind us that even celestial beings need caffeine,
companionship,
and a place to rest their wings.

FOREWORD

Welcome, book-loving tea and coffee aficionados!

If you've wandered into this little book, you're probably someone who believes—or at least suspects—that magic hides in ordinary places.

In teashops.

In cafés.

In the steam rising from a cup.

In the quiet moments between one world and the next.

These stories have always lived there.

Maggie McCready brews intuition into every pot of tea.

Larissa learns that even archangels need caffeine to survive Earth.

Phineas drinks like a fallen star remembering how to rise.

Somewhere between them all, a universe of warmth, wonder, and gentle chaos unfolds.

This book is a doorway—a playful, cosy, mythic introduction to the cafés and teashops that anchor these worlds. Inside, you'll meet the angels, explore their favourite brews, peek behind the counter, and discover why tea and coffee may be the most universal languages of all.

So, pour yourself something warm.

Settle in.

And wander between worlds.

Books, brews, bakes and blessings,

Melody R. Green

Contents

PART I

WELCOME TO THE CELESTIAL CAFE

When you arrive at the Celestial Café, you'll feel the difference straight away.

From a human perspective, you'll sense the glow—a harmony unlike anything you've seen or heard on Earth. The light sparkles and shimmers. The air feels warm but not dense, like a perfect summer's day. Everywhere you look, there is a feeling of cleanliness that is bright rather than clinical, and the aromas... Like the best on Earth—magnified a thousandfold.

It's as though every follicle of your nose and every taste receptor of your tongue has joined together to recognise flavours you've dreamt of but never experienced.

But as overwhelming as this can be for humans, it is simply *the café* for the angelic realm. They treat it the same way you would—like your favourite place for coffee or tea. So rather than spend time eulogising this sacred space, let's watch how the angels move within it.

Larissa stands at the café entrance reading the notice pinned to the door...

OFFICIAL STATEMENT FROM THE ARCHANGELIC COUNCIL

(As transcribed by Metatron, reluctantly approved by Michael, and enthusiastically shouted by Sandalphon)

To the humans of Earth,

It has come to our attention that many of you have expressed interest in sampling the beverages consumed within the Celestial Realms—including, but not limited to:

- Maple Caramel Serenity
- Garden of Stillness Green Tea
- IGNITE!
- Archangeli-cino
- Rose-Quartz Infusion
- Midnight Herbal Veil
- Rainbow Latte
- Seraphic Triple Shot
- The Divine Drip
- The Halo Roast
- Whisky-Smoked Lapsang Soulshong

After careful review (and one regrettable incident involving an over-caffeinated cherub attempting to reorganise the moon), the Council issues the following clarification:

1. Celestial Brews Are Not Available on Earth

Our beverages are crafted using:

- starlight
- harmonic resonance
- phoenix-ember roasts
- cosmic botanicals
- and, in one case, the emotional aftermath of a meteor shower.

These ingredients are not currently export-approved for the mortal plane.

Attempts to replicate them have resulted in:

- spontaneous levitation
- prophetic dreams
- mild time dilation
- and one human briefly speaking fluent Seraphic.

Therefore, for your safety (and ours), celestial brews remain Heaven-exclusive.

2. Recommended Earth-Approved Alternatives

While you cannot access our beverages, we wholeheartedly endorse the following earthly artisans, whose creations most closely echo the spirit of our own:

Madame Flavour Teas (www.madameflavour.com)

Elegant, soulful, beautifully blended.

Gabriel personally approves their calming frequencies.

On Earth, Michael choses **Grey de Luxe** in public. But he reaches for **Rooibos Mint Choc** when he thinks no one is looking.

Chilli Coffee Australia (www.chillicoffee.com.au)

Bold, vibrant, ethically crafted.

Sandalphon insists their roasts "have proper backbone."

Phineas describes them as "acceptable mortal fire."

These earthly brews will not cause levitation, prophecy, or dimension-shifting—but they will bring comfort, clarity and joy, which is the whole point of beverage magic.

3. A Note from the Archangels

"We invented tea and coffee. It was the only way we survived Earth."

— *Signed by every Archangel, including the ones who pretend they don't drink caffeine in any shape or form.*

Larissa took a deep breath. She was an angel, in training for sure, but that meant she could have a beverage at this café.

She picked up the beverage menu from the table near the door. It was divided into three parts.

CELESTIAL CAFÉ MENU

HEAVENLY COFFEE

Archangeli-cino
The Divine Drip
Seraphic Triple Shot
The Rainbow Latte
The Halo Roast

HEAVENLY TEAS

Michael's Maple Caramel Serenity
Gabriel's Garden of Stillness
Haniel's Rose-Quartz Infusion
Azreal's Midnight Herbal Veil
Raphael's Restorative Leaf
Israfel's Chromatic Bloom

Whisky-Smoked Lapsang Soulshong
Uriel's Lantern Tea

UNCATEGORISED:

IGNITE!

Sandalphon's brew. His only brew.

The highest caffeine hit in the known universe.
Served in a 600ml espresso cup.
Not tea. Not coffee. Not negotiable.
Engineered to:

- wake dormant timelines
- jump-start stalled destinies
- and power beings who work directly with Earth's density.

Drinking it may cause:

- spontaneous grounding
- seismic confidence
- and the sudden urge to get things *done.*

Warning:

Not served to humans.
Not served to angels with delicate nervous systems.
Never offered twice.

Larrisa wondered exactly how strong it might be, and whether she could handle it.

Before she got much further though, Michael strode towards her. "Sorry I'm late, there was a kerfuffle with a human's exit visa."

"Oh, what?"

"Trying to leave too early. It's wonderful that souls want to incarnate, but they must follow the procedure." He shook his head in disbelief. "Are you ready for the Celestial Café Special, Larissa?"

"I'm willing to try it." Larissa smiled, but as she went to move forward, a noisy group of cherubs swept by, chattering and giggling like wayward toddlers.

"Now settle down, cherubs." Israfel smiled joyfully, her energy sparkling over them like rainbow-coloured stardust.

A cheeky cherub spoke up from the back. "We'd like a 50ml Ignite! Please?"

Israfel stepped back, shocked. "You know you can't have one of those, even if it is only 50ml. But her eyes twinkled as she said, "Look at your own menu for your choices please." And they crowded around the Cherub Menu Card, specifically designed for small hands and constitutions.

CHERUB DRINKS MENU

NB: Cherubs are encouraged to remember that curiosity is admirable, enthusiasm is natural, and restraint is learned. The following beverages have been approved to support observation, learning, and gentle exploration.

The Angel Tea House blend

Garden of Stillness Green Tea

The Archangeli-cino

Celestial Hot Chocolate

NOT FOR CHERUBS

The following items are **not suitable** and will not be served:

Sandalphon's IGNITE!

Any coffee described as 'mission-grade', 'galactic', 'double', or 'character-building'.

Anything suggested with the words: *Just try it!*

Larissa watched the cherubs carefully choosing from their menu and felt a familiar warmth in her chest. "It matters," she said. "Letting them belong without overwhelming them."

"I agree, Larissa. Why don't you grab us a table and I'll get the coffees."

Michael set one Archangeli-cino down in front of Larissa and placed his Maple Caramel Serenity on the table for him, as if this were the most normal thing in Heaven.

Larissa took one sip, smiled, and then quietly pushed it back. "It's charming," she said. "But it's not...mission." She stood, returned to the counter, and moved behind it without asking; adjusted the grind, recalibrated the brew, and worked with the kind of focus that didn't rush.

Metatron, who had been very deliberately *not* intervening, watched closely.

When Larissa lifted the cup, inhaled once, and nodded—satisfied—he spoke. "You understand alignment," he said.

Larissa froze. "I just know what works."

Metatron regarded the machine, the cup, and the result. "That," he said, "is precisely the qualification." He paused, then added, "Heaven has been importing beverages. What we have lacked is a brewer."

Larissa blinked. "A... brewer?"

"Mistress of the Brew," Metatron corrected. "You'll introduce new blends as needed. Signature drinks. Adjustments. Safeguards."

He promptly sent her a communiqué covering her terms of employment, hours and tools of her trade. These were:

1) access to the Celestial Café all hours,

2) access to any ingredient deemed necessary to build flavour profiles for individuals or groups, and

3) the Brewer's Tablet to record all beverage ingredient ratios and trial notes, as requested by Metatron in the execution of her duty.

From the corner, Phineas looked up. "Oh, this is going to be fun," he said.

Metatron's gaze slid toward him. "For you," he said evenly, "it will be supervised." And then turned back to her. "What are you calling your brew, Larissa?"

She thought for a moment and said, "Inspiration Espresso." And then walked back to the table where Michael sat.

As Larissa enjoyed her Inspiration Espresso, she asked Michael, "How did tea and coffee end up in heaven, Michael?"

"You want the truth?" Michael said, taking his tea with an expression that suggested the tea was doing most of the work.

Larissa nodded. "Yes, please."

Michael's mouth twitched. "We didn't always have them."

"We had Ambrosia," Larissa said, remembering the luminous drink that appeared after...several incidents.

"Exactly. Which was fine," Michael said. "Until harmony got *comfortable*."

Larissa blinked. "Comfortable?"

"Heaven became so peaceful that urgency dissolved," Michael admitted. "When Father asked for a mission, most of us said yes—sincerely—and then promptly forgot."

Larissa stared. "Angels forgot?"

"Not our finest era," Michael agreed. "Metatron called it 'a developmental lull.' Sandalphon called it 'a problem' and went exploring."

"And came back with IGNITE," Larissa whispered, as if the word itself might wake something dangerous.

Michael nodded once. "Harrar. A kingdom that grows coffee with ceremonies that make the beans...enthusiastic."

"So, Metatron imported coffee?"

"He negotiated," Michael corrected, "with Olympus first. Zeus insisted they invented coffee."

Larissa smiled despite herself. “Of course he did.”

“Metatron also visited Shamballah for tea and Ikonius for cacao.” Michael’s eyes warmed slightly. “Cacao is reserved for celebrations. Heaven has rules.”

“And now we have a café,” Larissa said, looking around.

“And now we remember our missions,” Michael replied. “Mostly.”

Larissa narrowed her eyes. “Mostly?”

Michael’s tone went dry. “Uriel has a scroll for you. He’s making it homework.”

Larissa turned and Uriel stood bearing an ancient scroll, a smirk on his face. “This is compulsory study. You will be marked on this one.”

THE SCROLL OF CELESTIAL BEVERAGE HISTORY

As Compiled by Uriel, Dean of Angel School
(Required Reading for Mission-Ready Beings)

I. ON THE AGE OF AMBROSIA

Before the introduction of tea, coffee, and cacao, the angelic realms sustained themselves on **Celestial Ambrosia**. This substance was sufficient for harmony, coherence, and joy. It was not sufficient for remembrance.

Note in the margin:
Harmony without engagement leads to drift.

II. ON THE DEVELOPMENTAL LULL

As Heaven grew increasingly harmonious, urgency softened. Missions were accepted sincerely—and then forgotten. This was not rebellion. Nor was it negligence.

It was a predictable outcome of systems without friction.

III. ON THE FOUR BEVERAGE KINGDOMS

Olympus

Ruled by Zeus, who maintains that coffee was invented by his court. This claim is disputed, documented, and allowed to stand for diplomatic reasons.

Marginal correction: Volume is not evidence.

Harrar

A realm where coffee is cultivated through ceremony and concentration, producing beans of exceptional potency. Access is restricted. Excess is common.

Cross-reference:
See Sandalphon. Repeatedly.

Shamballah

Gardens devoted to tea, grown as a practice of stillness,

clarity, and timing. The cultivation itself is considered part of the teaching.

Relevance: Angels need these qualities to effectively carry out their duties.

Ikonius

Source of celestial cacao, reserved strictly for rites of celebration and completion.

Important: Cacao is not motivational. It is commemorative.

IV. ON THE BEVERAGE ACCORDS

Metatron negotiated the importation of coffee, tea, and cacao as **instruments**, not indulgences.

Tea was designated for integration.

Coffee for clarity.

Cacao for celebration.

IGNITE was classified separately.

Margin annotation: IGNITE is not a beverage. It is a decision.

V. ON BREWERS AND GOVERNANCE

Importation alone did not resolve imbalance. It became evident that Heaven required not only supply, but discernment. Thus, the role of **Mistress of the Brew** was established.

Addendum: Mastery is demonstrated through proportion, not potency.

DEAN'S FINAL NOTE:

Read this scroll carefully:

Intention alone does not complete an assignment.

Beverages are tools, not rewards.

Misuse results in paperwork.

You will not be examined on dates. You will be observed for application.

Larissa rolled up the scroll and placed it under her arm. She would need to study it more thoroughly later.

"Thank you for the history lesson, Michael, but for now I have homework and need to put some time into my new role as the Mistress of the Brew. I'll catch you soon." She rose from the table, taking the coffee cup with her to the counter. She picked up a copy of the menu and left for her study room.

Michael found Metatron where he usually did—present without appearing to be anywhere in particular.

"She's on my ray," Michael said without preamble.

Metatron inclined his head. "I am aware."

Michael folded his wings in slightly, a gesture few noticed and fewer understood. "I've watched her step into responsibility quickly." He continued, "I want to be sure the weight of it isn't more than she intended to carry."

Metatron regarded him steadily. "She was not assigned the role."

"I know," Michael said. "She claimed it."

"Correct," Metatron replied. "Through discernment."

Michael exhaled—not doubt, exactly, but care. "She holds Phineas steady. That alone carries consequence."

Metatron's tone remained even. "She does not hold him steady. She regulates the system around him."

A pause.

"That distinction matters," Metatron added.

Michael considered this. "She still needs room to be herself."

"She has it," Metatron said. "She asks questions before she acts. That is not the mark of burden, it is the mark of mastery."

Michael's shoulders eased. "And if she falters?"

Metatron's gaze softened—barely perceptibly. "Then the system adjusts. As it always does."

Another pause.

"You raised her well," Metatron said.

Michael smiled, just slightly. "I'll tell her you said that."

Metatron allowed the smallest flicker of amusement. "I would prefer you didn't."

When Larissa returned to her desk, she was curious to learn all she could about the Beverage Accord and found this excerpt in the archives under *The Scroll of Practical Interventions.* The important section stated the following:

THE BEVERAGE ACCORDS (OR THE INTRODUCTION OF TEA, COFFEE AND CACAO TO HEAVEN)

When it became apparent that harmony alone did not sustain remembrance, Metatron was tasked with identifying a corrective measure.

He travelled first to **Harrar**, where coffee was cultivated with deliberate ceremony and guarded attentiveness. The potency of the brew was undeniable, though its use required discernment. Sandalphon, dispatched to assess its viability, returned energised, decisive, and unwilling to stop.

This was noted.

Metatron therefore sought a **regulated source,** and so travelled onward to **Olympus**. Zeus received him with enthusiasm and thunder.

Claims were made.

Credit was demanded.

Attributions were contested.

Metatron listened without interruption.

When Zeus paused—as all eventually do—Metatron spoke.

"This is not a question of invention," he said. "It is a question of application."

Terms were set. Coffee would be imported not as indulgence, but as **instrument**.

Strength would be moderated.

Use would be intentional.

Excess would not be encouraged.

Zeus agreed, believing he had won.

Metatron did not correct him.

On his return journey, Metatron visited **Shamballah**, where tea was cultivated as a practice of stillness and clarity, and **Ikonius**, where celestial cacao was reserved strictly for rites of celebration and completion.

Thus, the Beverage Accords were formed.

Tea for integration.

Coffee for clarity.

Cacao for celebration.

IGNITE! was classified separately.

Later that evening, Maggie and Larissa had a conversation about the differences and virtues of coffee and tea that is as old as time—regardless of where in the universe you live.

Maggie: I still don't understand how you drink something that smells like burnt determination.

Larissa: It's called coffee, Maggie. It's how angels stay awake during cosmic briefings.

Maggie: Tea has kept humans awake for centuries.

Larissa: Tea whispers. Coffee shouts. Sometimes the universe needs volume.

Maggie: Tea is gentle magic. It soothes the soul.

Larissa: Coffee is rocket-fuel. It launches the soul.

Maggie: You know you can ascend without espresso, right?

Larissa: Can I though?

Maggie: Hmm...

Larissa: Exactly.

PART II

MEET THE ANGELS (AND THEIR DRINKS)

Over the next few days, Larissa worked on expanding the standard coffee menu until she felt she'd got it right, and then continued with tea. Her Brew Tablet was getting decidedly fuller with brew recipes, commentary, and insightful brew questions about ingredients and flavourings.

After all, Starlight Dust might not interact with all customers positively. She would need to do some testing. She looked over her revamped menu. It was almost complete

Larissa discovered very quickly that being Mistress of the Brew was not the same as being inspired.

Some blends arrived fully formed—a sudden clarity, a felt *yes*—as though they had been waiting patiently for her to notice them. Others resisted her completely.

Phineas' did.

She tried, at first, to approach it like any other problem.

She noted his preferences: strength, intensity, a fondness for anything that crackled or smoked. She sketched combinations on her tablet—darker roasts, sharper notes, even a reckless flirtation with Harrar beans that she abandoned almost immediately.

None of it felt right. She brewed. She tasted. She frowned.

Every test cup was...competent. Which was precisely the problem. Phineas was not competent. He was a contradiction. Fire and remorse. Destruction turned deliberately toward creation. An angel who had fallen not out of malice, but momentum. His fire had learned restraint, chaos had found a reason to stay, he who had once destroyed had risen again because love had given him somewhere to put his intensity, and something worth slowing for.

Larissa stared at the latest attempt and sighed. "Too much heat," she murmured. "Not enough meaning."

From the other side of the café, Phineas watched her with exaggerated patience as if he had all the centuries in the world which—annoyingly—he did.

"You know," he said, leaning against the counter, "I'm starting to take this personally."

She smiled without looking up. "You should. This matters."

He blinked. "It does?" Phineas' smirk faltered, just for a moment.

"Yes," she said simply. "Because this isn't about coffee. It's about who you are now." Larissa continued, softer, "You're not a warning label. You're a transformation."

Something shifted in the air—the kind of shift that happens when truth is spoken without drama.

Phineas looked away at first, as if the ceiling suddenly required his full attention. Then he stopped and grinned. He liked that description. He felt...seen.

Later that evening, after the café had quietened and the light had softened into its evening glow, Larissa sat alone with her Brew Tablet. She wasn't writing recipes now, just questions.

What tempers fire without extinguishing it?

What holds chaos without caging it?

What does redemption taste like?

She closed her eyes and let herself think not of Phineas the troublemaker, but Phineas the beloved. She thought of Phineas' laugh—too loud, too bright—and the way it sometimes covered something tender. She thought of how he hovered at the edges of the Archangelic fold, pretending he didn't care about belonging.

And then she thought about the *one* thing that had changed everything. Love hadn't softened him into weakness. Love had redirected Phineas' power. It had focused him.

Larissa brewed herself a small cup of Inspiration Espresso and drank it slowly, letting the warmth still her mind the way a hand calmed a frightened animal.

The warmth settled.

Clarity arrived—not as words, but as sensation.

Fire, yes. But fire with purpose, not wild.

Heat that transforms, not consumes. A bitterness deepened into richness. A finish that lingered like forgiveness.

Her fingers began moving across the tablet.

Storm-heat roasting. A volcanic note—not sharp, but honest. Cinnamon for courage. Chilli for edge. Cacao smoke for memory.

She paused.

And then—the name arrived so cleanly it felt like it had always been waiting.

Inferno.

Not destruction. The moment fire learns restraint.

Larissa sat back, heart oddly calm, and realised she was smiling.

"Of course," she whispered. "That's what you are."

When Phineas returned to Heaven—healed, whole, reconciled—the angels had offered him every celestial coffee. He rejected them all. Now it was time to see if her brew was on point.

Sandalphon and Michael stood either side of Phineas, waiting to see the impact of his signature brew.

The archangels crowded into the café, intent on witnessing the first sip. Larissa made the coffee and presented it in a 300ml espresso cup and then stood anxiously, the other side of the counter.

"Alright, chaos-boy. Take a good mouthful." Sandalphon grinned.

"What is it?' Phineas asked suspiciously.

"Your destiny in a cup," said Sandalphon.

"It's called Inferno," Larissa murmured.

"It's called Phineas' Inferno," corrected Michael.

Phineas raised his eyebrow. "Dramatic. I approve."

"Just drink it!" said Larissa impatiently.

Phineas took a sip. "Oh... Oh, this is..." He took another sip. "This is the taste of my entire character arc when I discovered love." He looked intently at Larissa.

"It is...fitting," declared Michael.

"It tastes like fire, redemption and questionable decisions," said Phineas.

"Exactly!" agreed Sandalphon.

"So...you like it?" asked Larissa.

"I LOVE IT. THIS IS WHO I AM NOW!" shouted Phineas.

"At least it is not Harrar," quipped Michael drily.

"HEY," said Sandalphon as he nudged Michael in the ribs.

When they left the café, Larissa got out her brew tablet and wrote up the description in her completed menu.

PHINEAS' INFERNO

A smoky, ember-roasted celestial brew, infused with volcanic cinnamon, molten cacao, chilli and star-salt. Chaotic, passionate, reborn. A fallen star remembering how to rise. Excellent for remembering destiny, redemption, and dramatic declarations of love.

Yes, it was complete.

A moment later, Michael reappeared. "Thank you, Larissa. It suits him—the fire, the warmth and the depth."

"You're proud of him," Larissa realised.

"I always was. Even when he was...difficult."

Larissa grinned. "He's still difficult."

"Yes. But now he is difficult with purpose." He saluted her and left the café.

The next day, as Larissa prepped for her meeting with Metatron, she overheard Sandalphon and Phineas squabbling.

"So! You've finally given up on that Whisky-Smoked Lapsang stuff you were drinking?" asked Sandalphon.

"That's Whisky-Smoked Lapsang Soulshong to you Sandalphon, and at least it's not that turbo charged Harrar you drink!"

"There's nothing wrong with Harrar!"

"It's definitely yours, that's for sure! Your...giant-mug, giant-ego, giant-energy brew."

"And now you've got your own—Cute!"

"It's not cute. It's infernal," Phineas said.

"It's adorable. Look at you with your little volcanic-roast identity crisis!" Sandalphon mocked.

"I will set your mug on fire."

"You say that like it's a threat," grinned Sandalphon.

At that point, Larissa blocked out their chatter and went back to preparing her report for Metatron.

Late in the day the café was closed—before the night shift came on—and Larissa was ready to give her report. She left a message for Metatron and went to prepare his signature coffee. He hadn't tried it yet and she hoped he'd like it.

He didn't walk in, he simply appeared. "Is this for me?"

"Yes," said Larissa, watching as he lifted the demitasse cup to his nose to smell, and then to his lips.

He took the first sip and closed his eyes. A gentle smile appeared around his mouth. "Yes, perfect to the last microgram... Well done, Larissa."

Larissa smiled and presented him with the updated menus.

Metatron read without interruption.

Larissa sat opposite him, hands loosely folded, resisting the urge to fill the silence. She'd learned that silence was not absence with Metatron—it was process.

He reached the end of the document and didn't look up.

"You've reduced the menu," he said.

"Yes," Larissa replied. "Not in variety. In impulse."

Metatron's eyes lifted then, sharp but not unkind.

"Explain."

"Coffee creates momentum," she said. "Tea creates integration. Too many choices at the wrong moment encourages stimulation, instead of clarity."

Metatron nodded once. "You've restricted Ambrosia."

"I have," Larissa said. "It shouldn't be reachable through habit."

A pause.

"And the Cornetto?" he asked.

"It's a memory," she said quietly. "Not a drink."

Metatron returned his attention to the page. "You've assigned purpose to every brew."

"Yes."

"Even the celebratory ones."

"Especially those."

He set the document down. "This menu will reduce overconsumption," he said. "It will stabilise nervous systems. It will lower incidents involving cherubs."

Larissa smiled despite herself. "Good."

"But..." Metatron continued, "it will also slow certain beings."

She didn't argue.

"Phineas," he said.

"Yes."

Another silence—shorter this time.

"You have not tried to control him," Metatron observed.

"No," Larissa said. "I've tried to pace the world around him."

Metatron considered this.

"That is governance," he said at last. "Not enforcement."

He paused, then added, almost conversationally, "You've left room for humour."

Larissa tilted her head. "Intentionally."

"Morale improves when beings feel seen," Metatron said. "Even when they disagree."

"I would like your thoughts on including your white tea for the cherubs—it might help them feel more included, able to take on more responsibility. What do you think?"

He paused in thought. "Let's give it a trial run. If it works, we can keep it. If not, it will need to be removed."

"Of course."

He made a brief note on his phone. "This menu is approved," he said.

Larissa exhaled.

"Provisionally."

She met his gaze again. "Yes?"

"Systems that adapt are permitted to continue," Metatron said. "Systems that calcify are replaced."

He handed the document back to her. "Proceed."

As she turned to leave, he added, "And Larissa?"

She stopped.

"Thank you," he said. "For remembering that clarity does not require severity."

She smiled—not brightly, but steadily—and removed the cups to the kitchen.

Behind her, Metatron made one more notation and then left.

Larissa sat, quietly re-arranging the menu. She wanted it ready for the next shift.

It was divided into three parts. The standard coffees and teas, the specialised brews and those that stood outside the two. Her instinct told her that Phineas' brew should be added to this as a matter of caution.

Finally, there was the Cherub's Menu, with the additions.

She was pleased with her efforts.

CELESTIAL CAFÉ MENU

STANDARD CAFÉ BREWS

The Seraphic Slow Brew

A long, meditative pour-over, used to calm celestial nerves and cultivate patience. Best suited for difficult missions and periods of emotional turbulence.

The Divine Doppio

A double espresso taken before any celestial assignment. Supports clarity, confidence, and forward momentum.

Side effects may include mild halo vibration.

The Revelation Ristretto

A tightly focused, highly concentrated brew used when single-pointed clarity is essential.

Often leads to unexpected insight and decisive understanding.

This is the most *focused* coffee on the standard menu.

The Ascension Affogato

A coffee experience offered to acknowledge exceptional service. An espresso poured over vanilla ice cream and served when an angel has exceeded the expectations of a mission.

This is not preparation, but recognition.

The Mending Marocchino

A blend of cacao and coffee used for emotional repair. Often served after heartbreak, disappointment, or overwhelming paperwork.

The Compassionate Cappuccino

Warm, gentle, and softening. Traditionally served in the morning, when softness is still possible. Used before delivering difficult messages to humans.

The Brew of Becoming

A symbolic cup shared when an angel steps into a new phase of growth. Rarely repeated. Favoured by Larissa.

The Cornetto

A ceremonial sip combining coffee and a trace of Celestial Ambrosia. Offered only on rare occasions, when an angel has interacted deeply with human density and requires gentle re-alignment. This is not a beverage, but a moment. Served as a single, measured sip—never more. Intended to restore coherence without stimulation and to remind the drinker of what came before coffee.

Restricted use.
Not listed on the public menu.

ARCHANGEL-SPECIFIC SIGNATURE COFFEE BLENDS

Zasphiel's Cosmic Cold Brew

Steeped in starlight for seventy-two celestial hours with a trace of meteor dust. Designed to harmonise galactic encounters and extended council duties.

Azrael's Gentle Wake-Up

A soft, low-acid coffee with notes of chocolate and smoke. Often consumed with compassion and restraint.

Metatronic Espresso

Measured to the microgram. Sharpens the mind to a knife's edge. Precise. Potent. Perfect. Consumed only when Herculean tasks are required. When Metatron drinks this, tasks organise themselves.

Tzadkiel's Mercy Mocha

A milk-rich cacao coffee infused with compassion. Used after difficult missions or emotional breakthroughs. A favourite of Tzadkiel.

Gabriel's Second Notice Espresso

Sharp and clarifying, like a trumpet blast. Designed for moments when messages must be delivered clearly and without delay. Created as a gift from Larissa.

Inspiration Espresso

Larissa's own blend. Mission-grade. Alignment-based. Served when the next step appears in a single flash. Not caffeine—clarity.

Haniel's Heartspark Cappuccino

A velvety cappuccino with a bright, joyful lift. Foam tends to form hearts (even when no one asks it to). Encourages harmony, confidence, and singing in tune. Best served during seraphim practice—and after a long day of herding radiant cats.

Raphael's Restorative Flat White

Low-acid, gentle strength, quietly medicinal. Tastes like 'you'll be okay' without having to say it out loud. Supports recovery, integration, and nervous systems that have seen too much. Often ordered after missions and never rushed.

The Dean's Double (also known as Uriel's Cortado)

Small, strong, and designed for long lessons. A cortado with a clean finish—nothing wasted, nothing excessive. Improves focus, retention, and the patience required to teach beings who think they're already enlightened. Not recommended for cherubs unless their mentor approves. (They will not.)

BLEND UNDER ADVISEMENT

Sandalphon's IGNITE!

Phineas' Inferno

A smoky, ember-roasted celestial brew infused with volcanic cinnamon, molten cacao, chilli and star-salt. Chaotic, passionate, reborn. A fallen star remembering how to rise. Excellent for remembering destiny, redemption, and dramatic declarations of love.

ARCHANGEL-SPECIFIC SIGNATURE TEA BLENDS

Phineas' Whisky-Smoked Lapsang Soulshong

Tastes like a forest fire with opinions.

Zasphiel's Stellar Infusion

A dark, elegant tea with star anise and cacao husk. Ancient, expansive, and contemplative.

Israfel's Chromatic Bloom

A radiant infusion of hibiscus, rose, and butterfly pea flower. Shifts colour as it steeps.

Metatron's Perfectly Measured White Tea

Available **with your mentor's permission**. Delicate, precise, and subtly clarifying. Supports understanding of process, timing, and why not everything needs to happen at once. Not to be rushed.

CHERUBS BEVERAGE MENU

NB: Cherubs are encouraged to remember that curiosity is admirable, enthusiasm is natural, and restraint is learned. The following beverages have been approved to support observation, learning, and gentle exploration.

The Angel Tea House blend

Warm, comforting, and quietly magical. A familiar taste of home that supports patience, attentiveness, and sitting still long enough to notice what matters.

The most frequently ordered drink among cherubs. For good reason.

Garden of Stillness Green Tea

Soft, luminous, and calming. Encourages listening, message-adjacent learning, and thoughtful silence. Favoured during observation shifts and after excitement.

Metatron's Perfectly Measured White Tea

Available **with your mentor's permission**. Delicate, precise, and subtly clarifying. Supports understanding of process, timing, and why not everything needs to happen at once. Not to be rushed.

The Archangeli-cino

Available **only with mentor supervision**. Foamy, uplifting, and mildly chaotic. Often ordered as a first experience of coffee. Teaches discernment through experience. Often recommended as a first-mission drink before one graduates to stronger alignments. Second cups are not advised.

Celestial Hot Chocolate

Served with foam, warmth, and encouragement. No caffeine required to feel included. Always approved. Restorative, grounding, and morale-boosting. Recommended when unsure, overwhelmed, or after listening to Phineas for more than thirty seconds. *Not Ceremonial strength.*

NOT FOR CHERUBS

The following items are **not suitable** and will not be served:

Sandalphon's IGNITE!

Phineas' Inferno

Any coffee described as 'mission-grade' 'galactic', 'double', or 'character-building'

Anything suggested with the words: *Just try it!*

CLOSING NOTE from METATRON

- All beverages are offered with intention.
- Excess is discouraged.
- Curiosity is welcomed.
- Discernment is expected.

Some days were just like that in heaven. It seemed as though everything happened at once, as though collectively the angels went from one crisis to another. Today was this day. Larissa hoped they had enough tea and coffee for the fallout... Maybe she should let Metatron know. *Who do I speak to about such things?* she wondered.

But before she could make a decision, she was run off her feet...

Gabriel stood at the counter, wings drawn in tighter than usual, eyes fixed on the menu as if it had personally disappointed him.

"I delivered the message," he said calmly. "Clearly. Repeatedly. With signs."

Azrael slid onto the stool beside him and ordered without looking. "Coffee."

"Oh, you look battle-weary. I've just finished creating your personalized brew—it seems like serendipitous timing. Would you like to try it?" Larissa asked.

Gabriel sighed. It was the kind of sigh that carried centuries of patience and the faint hope that someone, somewhere, might eventually listen.

They nodded as Gabriel continued. "They thanked me. One of them wrote it down."

"And then?" Azrael asked.

"They did the opposite."

Azrael accepted his cup when it arrived—**Azrael's Gentle Wake-Up**, warm and unassuming. He took a sip and briefly closed his eyes.

"Humans," he said, "are deeply committed to experience."

Gabriel finally gave in and ordered **Gabriel's Second Notice Espresso**. Larissa raised an eyebrow but said nothing.

"I don't enjoy coffee," Gabriel said as it was placed in front of him. "It sharpens things."

"That's the point," Azrael replied mildly. "You're not here to enjoy it."

Gabriel took one reluctant sip. His expression shifted—not displeased, but alert.

"Fine," he conceded. "One cup."

Azrael smiled faintly. "Careful. That's how it starts."

Across the room, a cherub glanced at them and quietly put the menu down.

PART III

CHAOS, CALAMITY AND MISHAP

THE NEXT MORNING, LARISSA entered the café to find it full to the rafters, conversations and laughter filling the space delightfully. Even the Seraphim were drinking coffee. She paused, wondering if that was allowed. She hadn't thought of giving them their own menu.

Perhaps she should check with Haniel about that.

She made a note on her tablet for later.

Haniel was passing the rehearsal room when she stopped.

The Seraphim was meant to be rehearsing. Instead, they were...vibrating.

Not in the good, luminous, harmonically aligned way either—but in the jittery, overbright, slightly out-of-phase manner that suggested someone had ignored a very clear advisory notice.

Haniel walked into the room and stood in the centre, hands loosely clasped, smiling with the kind of patience usually reserved for herding particularly enthusiastic cats.

"All right," she said gently. "From the beginning."

They began to sing.

The sound was impressive. Powerful. Radiant. Slightly alarming.

A high note wobbled, split, then reassembled itself a fraction of a second too late. Another Seraph laughed mid-note and immediately apologised.

Haniel raised one eyebrow.

"Who," she asked mildly, "ordered coffee?"

There was a pause.

Several wings rustled.

One Seraph raised a tentative hand. "Phineas said it would help us project."

Haniel closed her eyes for a moment. "Of course he did."

She moved to the side table and quietly replaced the abandoned mugs with tall glasses of cool, shimmering liquid.

"No more coffee," she said, still smiling. "You're not here to *power* the sound. You're here to *become* it."

One of the Seraph swallowed. "But singing forever dries your throat."

Haniel nodded sympathetically. "Yes. Eternity can be very dehydrating."

She gestured to the glasses. "This will help. Hydration first. Harmony second. Ambition later."

They drank.

Almost immediately, the frantic edge softened. The air settled. Colours aligned. The next note—when it came—was clear, effortless, and so perfectly balanced it seemed to hang in the room on its own.

Haniel smiled properly this time.

"Better," she said. "Now—again. And this time, please trust that you don't need caffeine to be magnificent."

From the doorway, a cherub quietly crossed *Seraphic Triple Shot* off the menu.

Larissa was surprised to see Haniel later that morning.

"Did you hear the din from the rehearsal room?" Haniel asked, laughing.

"No," Larissa replied. "The noise here was quite strong enough. It would seem the new menu was successful."

"Possibly too successful."

"Oh?"

"The Seraphim admitted to having the *Seraphic Triple Shot*."

Larissa grimaced. "I removed that on purpose. I could see it was going to be too strong for them. I wonder how that happened?"

She pulled up the early-morning roster and then thumped her hand against her head.

"Oh no. Sandalphon was on shift."

Haniel smiled. "That would explain it."

"No wonder they were over-caffeinated. Are they all right now?"

"Yes. I rebalanced them with an extremely weak brew of Celestial Ambrosia—one drop of essence in a glass of cool spring water. It's excellent for throat problems. Gabriel and Israfel use it as well when they have extensive messages or translations to manage."

"Oh, I didn't know about that. May I have some for the café?"

"Certainly."

"I'll speak with Sandalphon and make sure there are no further mistakes. The Seraphic Cool Brew should be suitable for them. I'll update the menu." Larissa glanced up. "Can I get you anything, Haniel?"

Haniel considered this.

"I think," she said thoughtfully, "I might need a Seraphic Triple Shot myself. But only a very small cup."

A few days later, Michael arrived at the Celestial Café feeling battle-weary from a long night fighting demonic forces.

His usually pristine black wings were drawn in close to his body, feathers dulled and faintly singed at the edges. His full battle gear, normally immaculate, looked well lived in.

What he needed was quiet. Space. And a properly brewed cup of Maple Caramel Serenity Tea.

Instead, as he stepped into the otherwise empty café, he found Sandalphon on barista duty.

Michael sighed. Peace, it seemed, was not an option today.

"A rough night, Michael?" Sandalphon asked cheerfully, already reaching for a cup.

Michael closed his eyes briefly. "You'd better believe it. I'll take my usual, please."

Sandalphon studied him, then shook his head. "Looking at you, I'd say you need something stronger."

"No," Michael said firmly. "Alignment and stillness in the form of Maple Caramel Serenity is precisely the ticket."

Sandalphon lifted a six-hundred-millilitre coffee cup—which looked absurdly small in his massive hand. "Stillness is overrated. Give me an *Ignite!* any day. Bright. Bold. Alive." He grinned. "Like drinking sunlight that's had a bad idea."

Michael regarded him in silence.

"Tea," he said at last, "is subtle. Nuanced. It whispers wisdom."

"Coffee shouts it," Sandalphon replied, taking a heroic gulp. "Honestly, Michael—the rest of you, with the exception of Phineas—are such pussycats with your delicate little blends."

Michael raised an eyebrow. "Maple Caramel is not delicate. It is...harmonious."

"It's dessert in a cup."

"It is balanced."

"It's sugar with an identity crisis."

"At least my beverage doesn't require a fire extinguisher."

"That was one time," Sandalphon protested. "And the mug survived."

"Barely."

Sandalphon laughed. "Look, some of us ascend gently." He gestured at Michael's tea. "And some of us ascend at twelve hundred caffeine units per second."

"And some of us prefer not to vibrate through walls."

"Walls are optional."

"Not for the humans below," Michael replied dryly.

Sandalphon snorted. "Fine. I'll try your Maple Caramel tea."

He took a sip. Paused. Considered. "...Nope."

He immediately followed it with a massive swig of *Ignite!* "I need flavour that fights back."

"And I," said Michael calmly, "need beverages that do not threaten structural integrity."

"Agree to disagree."

"As always."

Sandalphon grinned. "But if you ever want to try a *real* drink, I'll make you an *Ignite!* triple-shot."

"If I ever require cardiac intervention," Michael said, lifting his cup, "I'll let you know. But thank you for the conversation, Sandalphon."

"Any time, Michael. Any time."

Michael took a long, quiet sip of his tea.

And slowly—very slowly—the universe realigned itself.

Larissa brewed his Maple Caramel Serenity the way he liked it and joined him at the table.

"There's something I've been wondering," she said. "If tea and coffee became tools in Heaven, how did they end up with humans?"

Michael smiled the kind of smile that suggested several centuries had just been condensed. "Ambition," he said. "Geography. And a great deal of borrowing."

Larissa waited.

"When humans began organising themselves," Michael continued, "certain powers felt the need to be *seen*. Mountains were useful for that."

"Mount Olympus," she said.

"Eventually," Michael agreed. "Height creates distance. Humans respond to it."

She made a brief note.

"Tea travelled differently," he went on. "Quietly. Along roads and through monasteries. It suited places that valued patience more than spectacle."

"Shamballah," Larissa said.

Michael inclined his head. "They always think long-term."

"And coffee?"

His expression shifted slightly. "Africa first. Guarded. Ceremonial. Shared carefully—until humans realised what it did."

"And cacao?"

"That arrived as celebration," Michael said. "For marking moments rather than sustaining them."

Larissa leaned back, thoughtful. "So the same practices—just adapted?"

"Humans rarely invent," Michael replied. "They remember. Eventually."

From nearby, Uriel cleared his throat. "This is not required reading," he said mildly. "But it *does* qualify for extra credit."

Larissa laughed and returned to her tablet, already sketching connections.

Somewhere in Heaven's accounting systems, a small notation updated itself.

What works in Heaven, it seemed, always found a way to become human.

Sometimes Larissa needed tea. She looked at the tea menu, but nothing made her heart quiver with joy. She closed her eyes briefly, a memory of long ago coming to her, a tea blend she used to drink when she was human. It was on the tip of her tongue, and she raced to her brewing room to test it out.

The name came first—Songfire Chai—and there it was, a melodic, spiced chai infused with musical resonance and emotional truth. Artistic, soulful, radiant. A warm chord played directly on the heart. Delightful for creativity, prophecy, and singing mortals back to themselves. Yes, this was the one.

Azrael and Tzadkiel stood to one side of the café door, watching.

"I have escorted souls through every imaginable chaos," Azrael said quietly, watching Phineas down another Phineas' Inferno. "But this... This I was not prepared for."

"We must show compassion," Tzadkiel agreed, hands clasped. "He is clearly overwhelmed."

"I CAN SEE SOUND," Phineas shouted joyfully. "I HAVE NEVER BEEN MORE ALIVE!"

"Perhaps compassion," Tzadkiel murmured, "from a distance."

"Oh, this is wonderful!" Haniel beamed. "He's like a comet with opinions."

Sandalphon lifted his 600ml cup of IGNITE! appreciatively. "Finally, someone who understands the power of a proper brew."

"This is your fault," Michael said flatly.

Sandalphon shrugged. "You're welcome."

Metatron opened his mouth—and froze as Phineas spotted him.

"METATRON," Phineas boomed, "I CAN HEAR THE UNIVERSE BREATHING."

Metatron turned to Michael. "Restrain your brother."

"I would rather fight a dragon."

"He is a dragon now," Sandalphon smirked. "A caffeinated one."

"Should we call Larissa?" Gabriel asked.

"She *made* the brew," Sandalphon said.

"Oh, I see," Gabriel said.

Michael took a steady breath and stepped beside Phineas. "You seem unsettled."

"I AM PERFECTLY SETTLED," Phineas grinned. "I AM THE DEFINITION OF SETTLED."

"You are shouting."

"I AM SPEAKING WITH PASSION."

"You are vibrating."

"I AM EXPRESSING MYSELF."

"And glowing," Michael added.

"I AM RADIANT."

Michael sighed. "Very well. Perhaps I should understand this beverage myself."

Phineas gasped, thrusting a fist into the air. "YES! TRY THE ARCHANGELI-CINO—NO!" He thrust out his hand to stop Michael. "ON SECOND THOUGHTS IT HAD BETTER BE DECAF. WE MUST BREAK YOU IN GENTLY."

Michael accepted the cup with dignified caution. "I do not require my life to be changed."

"You say that now."

He took a sip. "Oh."

"RIGHT?" Phineas leaned in.

"This is...unexpectedly pleasant."

"MICHAEL. THIS IS LIQUID DESTINY."

"It is invigorating."

"You're underselling it."

"I am being accurate."

"You're being Michael."

Michael sipped again. "I see why Larissa enjoys this."

"SHE IS A GENIUS. A CHAOS-BRINGER."

"She is...effective."

"She is my BELOVED."

"And my sister," Michael replied calmly. "This beverage is...efficient."

"MICHAEL. YOU ARE BUZZING."

"I am not buzzing."

"You are buzzing."

"I am..." Michael checked his aura. "...slightly elevated."

"WELCOME TO COFFEE."

Larissa arrived just before lunchtime.

The café was vibrating.

"Which one of you caused the dimensional tremors?" she asked.

Phineas lifted his mug. "NOT ME."

"It was him," Michael said serenely.

"TRAITOR."

"Michael," Larissa frowned. "You're glowing."

"I am mildly energised."

"HE'S BUZZING. HE'S FINALLY BUZZING."

"I am experiencing heightened clarity."

"That's what Phineas said before he tried to alphabetise the constellations."

"IT WAS A GOOD SYSTEM."

"It was chaos."

"I AM CHAOS."

"You were chaos," Michael said thoughtfully. "Now you are... structured chaos."

"Oh no," Larissa sighed. "Two caffeinated philosophers."

"WE SHOULD START A PODCAST."

"We should not."

"WE SHOULD."

"Both of you—sit. Water. Breathe. Stop vibrating."

"I CAN'T FEEL MY FACE."

"I can feel everything," Michael said, awed.

"Wonderful," Larissa muttered. "I'm babysitting cosmic toddlers."

"WE LOVE YOU."

"We appreciate your guidance."

Larissa reached for tea. "We're doing a detox."

"ABSOLUTELY NOT."

"I am...open to the possibility," Michael murmured.

Tzadkiel handed them herbal tea.

"It tastes like regret," Phineas said.

"It tastes...peaceful," Michael replied.

"You re-organised the archives by emotional resonance," Larissa said. "And you..." she said, pointing to Phineas, "you taught a meteor shower to tap dance."

"THEY LEARNED."

"They collided."

"BUT ARTISTICALLY."

Michael exhaled. "Perhaps we should reduce our intake."

"I WILL NOT BE CONTROLLED."

"You're not being controlled," Larissa said evenly. "You're being hydrated."

"...Fine," Phineas muttered. "One cup less."

"Per hour," Larissa said.

Michael returned to his normal self quickly after he'd hydrated and stood watching Phineas and Larissa from a distance. Phineas cradled his new, smaller mug of Inferno, his fire banked rather than blazing. Larissa stood nearby, not guarding, not correcting—simply present. For a long moment Michael said nothing and then turned quietly to Metatron. "She didn't restrain him."

"No," Metatron agreed.

"She didn't reduce him," Michael continued. "She didn't shame him into compliance."

Metatron's gaze remained steady. "She reminded him that he belongs."

Michael's wings shifted, the faintest sign of relief passing through him. "I spent a long-time believing order was the answer," he said. "Rules. Structure. Consequence."

"And they are," Metatron replied, "up to a point."

Michael nodded slowly. "But love reaches places rules never touch."

Metatron allowed a pause—not disagreement, but acknowledgment. "Yes," he said. "Love stabilises what rules merely contain."

Michael watched Phineas laugh at something Larissa said—softer now, less jagged. "That," Michael said, "is why he was allowed back."

"And why he stayed," Metatron replied.

They stood together for a while longer, not supervising, not intervening. Simply witnessing a system doing what it was designed to do.

And then Metatron lifted a small, unassuming device and made a brief note.

Michael glanced at it. "You keep records like that now?"

"Efficiency," Metatron replied. "Scrolls are slower."

Larissa had just finished rearranging the menu annotations when she felt it.

Not noise. Not chaos. Enthusiasm.

The kind that arrived before consequences.

She looked up from the counter.

A single cherub stood behind the espresso machine.

Wings tucked. Chin lifted. Expression earnest to the point of solemnity.

The cherub was wearing an apron.

It was on backwards.

Larissa opened her mouth.

Phineas, leaning against a nearby table, spoke first. "Oh, this is excellent," he said warmly. "I remember my first unsupervised decision."

The cherub beamed. "I'm helping."

"Helping how?" Larissa asked, crossing the room slowly.

"We're being baristas," the cherub said, gesturing behind them.

Only then did Larissa notice the others—three more cherubs clustered nearby, watching with reverent attention. One held a demitasse cup with both hands. Another had her Brew Tablet, turned sideways.

Phineas crouched slightly, lowering his voice conspiratorially. "Just a sip," he said. "Not a whole demitasse. You'll be fine."

Larissa stopped. "Phineas," she said calmly, "what brew is that?"

Phineas glanced at the machine. “Mine.”

Of course it was.

The cherub nodded proudly. “Phineas’ Inferno. We followed the description.”

Larissa inhaled once.

“Who is it for?” she asked.

The cherub smiled wider. “Everyone.”

The café hummed. Very softly.

Across the room, one Seraph—still fine-tuning after the earlier caffeine mishap—faltered mid-note. Her pitch slipped sideways, not collapsing, just...bending.

Raphael was beside her instantly.

“Easy,” he murmured. “Breathe with me.”

The hum deepened.

Uriel appeared near the counter, eyes narrowing.

“This,” he said mildly, “appears to be a scaling error.”

The cherub blinked. “We multiplied it.”

Phineas winced. “Ah.”

The brew completed itself.

Harmony overcorrected.

Chairs tipped gently, as if startled by their own existence. Mugs rattled, then stilled. The light shimmered—too aligned, like a chord held too long.

Larissa moved.

She shut down the machine, separated the brew into its component resonances, grounded the excess energy, and re-established containment with practiced ease.

The café exhaled. Silence fell.

The cherubs sat immediately, wings folded tight, cheeks flushed.

Raphael finished rebalancing the Seraph's pitch. "She's all right. Sensitive, not harmed."

"An instructive moment," Uriel observed.

Zasphiel arrived, surveyed the scene, and folded his arms. "This," he said sharply, "is precisely why restrictions exist."

No one looked up.

"You were given a menu. A warning. Mentors. Boundaries. And still you chose excess."

One cherub swallowed. "We just wanted to understand—"

"Understanding does not require recklessness," Zasphiel replied. "Nor does growth excuse disorder."

The word growth hung in the air.

Then Metatron spoke. "Actually," he said calmly, "it does."

The room shifted.

Raphael inclined his head slightly. "Understanding often arrives through experience."

"Correct," Metatron said.

He surveyed the scene without irritation or approval.

"Perfection is a misunderstanding," he said. "Nothing that lives is finished." He looked at the cherubs, not unkindly. "Growth is not a flaw. It is the point." He turned to Larissa. "You intervened before damage."

"Yes," she said. "But after learning."

Metatron nodded.

Larissa knelt in front of the cherubs. "Next time," she said gently, "you ask."

"Yes, Mistress of the Brew," they chorused.

Phineas raised a hand. "For the record, I did say sip."

Larissa gave him a look.

He lowered his hand.

A menu update appeared.

IDENTITY-SPECIFIC BREWS

Certain beverages are crafted for individual resonance profiles and must not be shared or scaled.

PORTION PROTOCOLS

- Demitasse cups are symbolic.
- Multiplication requires authorisation.
- 'For everyone' is not a measurement.

BARISTA ACCESS LEVELS

- Observation encouraged.
- Initiative welcomed.
- Scaling is advanced practice.

Larissa added a private annotation to her Brew Tablet:

Proposal:
Cherub Barista Apprenticeship—
observation-based, supervised, limited scope.

Metatron glanced at the note. "This warrants discussion," he said. "Not now."

"When?" Larissa asked.

"Soon," he replied. "No decisions. Only design."

She smiled. "That's all I'd ask."

"You are not preventing growth," Metatron said as he left. "You are pacing it."

Phineas studied the newly posted notice on the café wall and felt an irresistible urge to improve it.

Not because he craved rebellion or revolution—he'd explored those thoroughly already—but because he knew, from long experience, that morale responded far better to humour than obedience.

He produced his angelic pen, grinned to himself, and went to work.

CAFÉ RULES FOR BARISTAS

Written by Michael. Edited by Phineas. Posted on the wall. Constantly ignored.

1. Maintain order at all times.

Phineas: Tedious. Add "unless chaos is fun."

2. No open flames near the counter.

Phineas: (crosses out)

Open flames encouraged for dramatic effect.

3. Limit caffeine intake to safe levels.

Phineas: Define "safe."

4. Do not rearrange the sugar packets.

Phineas: They look better sorted by emotional intensity.

5. Respect all customers.

Phineas: Except Metatron when he's being pedantic.

6. Keep the café clean.
Phineas: Clean is subjective.
7. No celestial beverages for humans.
Phineas: Unless they sign a waiver.
Michael: NO.
8. Follow all instructions from management.
Phineas: Except when they're wrong.
9. No brewing after midnight.
Phineas: Midnight is a social construct.
10. Enjoy your work.
Phineas: Finally, a rule I like.

Later that day, Larissa noticed the cherubs giggling while reading the notice.

She chose not to intervene. Provided it didn't lead to inappropriate consumption—or spontaneous reality shifts—she was content to let it remain.

The amended rules reached Metatron within the hour. He read them carefully. Noted the annotations. Paused longest at the margins.

Then he made a brief entry on his phone and placed the notice precisely where it would be found again. Morale improved. No moons were rearranged. The system adjusted.

In the eternal present, the Celestial Café—under Larissa's guidance—had quietly become *the* place to be.

Which, in turn, meant the Kingdoms of Heaven were very keen to know why.

It wasn't long before the idea of a documentary was proposed. Then approved. Then *immediately* regretted by Michael.

Over the next few days, a small celestial film crew captured what they referred to as 'behind-the-scenes moments', attempting to assemble something that might explain the café's popularity—and allow its many admirers to express appropriate levels of awe.

What they got instead was this.

BEHIND THE SCENES AT THE CELESTIAL CAFÉ

The mockumentary

COLD OPEN

Camera pans to Sandalphon lifting a 600ml mug with one hand.

Sandalphon (to camera):
"This is a small."

SCENE ONE—MICHAEL'S INTERVIEW

Michael sits perfectly upright, hands folded, wings immaculate.

Michael:
"My role is to maintain order."

(beat)
"And prevent Phineas from setting the café on fire."
(another beat)
"Again."

Cut to Phineas flambéing cinnamon sticks with unnecessary enthusiasm.

SCENE TWO—LARISSA TRAINING A NEW ANGEL

Larissa stands patiently beside the espresso machine.

Larissa:

"Foam art is about intention.
You're not just pouring milk—you're pouring hope."

The new angel peers into the cup.

New Angel:

"...It looks like a blob."

Larissa:

"It's an *optimistic* blob."

SCENE THREE—METATRON'S ESPRESSO INCIDENT

Metatron examines the counter with forensic precision.

Metatron:

"The espresso machine has been moved three millimetres to the left."

Camera zooms in on Sandalphon, smirking.

SCENE FOUR—AZRAEL'S NIGHT SHIFT

The café lights are low. Everything is calm.

Azrael (softly):

"After midnight, we serve only herbal tea. And silence."

Cut to Haniel humming joyfully while making a latte.

Azrael:

"...Mostly silence."

SCENE FIVE—PHINEAS' CONFESSIONAL

Phineas leans casually against the counter.

Phineas:

"I don't have a caffeine problem. I have a caffeine calling."

Cut to Larissa calmly confiscating his third Inferno of the hour.

SCENE SIX—GABRIEL'S CUSTOMER SERVICE

Gabriel glows gently behind the counter.

Gabriel:

"Your tea is ready."

A fan customer blinks.

Customer:

"Why is it glowing?"

Gabriel:

"I'm happy."

ENDING SHOT

All the angels gather behind the counter.

Larissa:

"Okay, team—wings up. It's rush hour."

Camera pans to a long line of confused but delighted fans, stretching well past the door.

Fade out.

The documentary would eventually be edited, shared, and quietly archived. Long after the cameras were gone, the café remained much as it always did

Cups were rinsed. Counters wiped. Wings folded and unfolded with familiar ease. The hum of conversation softened into something quieter—a shared understanding that the work would begin again tomorrow.

Somewhere between the last cup and the first light, the Celestial Café returned to what it had always been.

A place to rest. A place to gather. A place where even angels were allowed to pause.

Because what mattered was never the footage or the fascination—it was the warmth, the welcome, and the simple truth that somewhere between worlds, there would always be a table set and a cup waiting.

And if you've found comfort here—in the warmth, the humour, the quiet moments between one world and the next—then this blessing is for you.

A Blessing for Those Who Wander Between Worlds

May your cups be warm,
your hearts steady,
and your kettles ever ready.
May you find sanctuary in small pauses,
magic in ordinary moments,
and guidance when you least expect it.
And when you wander—as all souls do—
may you always know where you can return—home.

—The Archangelic Council
Michael, Gabriel, Raphael, Uriel, Haniel, Tzadkiel, Azrael, Sandalphon, Metatron
(and Phineas, who insisted on adding "Chief Chaos Consultant," and was politely ignored)

The End

A NOTE FROM THE CELESTIAL CAFÉ

Thank you for spending time in the Celestial Café.

If you enjoyed these moments—the warmth, the banter, the quiet magic—this world began elsewhere, long before Larissa stepped behind the counter.

You can discover where it all began in the earlier novels set within this universe, where angelic guidance, human lives, and everyday rituals intertwine across time and place.

Wherever you choose to go next, the café doors remain open.

Books, brews, bakes and blessings,

Melody R. Green

ACKNOWLEDGEMENTS

No book comes together without the care and effort of many hands, and this one is no exception.

My sincere thanks go to **Sarah Lemcke** of *All in the Edit*, whose editorial insight and interior design work brought clarity and coherence to these pages. Nothing was too much trouble, and her thoughtful attention to detail helped this book become what it needed to be.

When I begin writing, I create the cover first—a small ritual that helps me focus. For this companion book, which sits between *Maggie McCready's Travelling Tarot Adventures* and *Larissa's Angelic Adventures*, I turned to **Jane Cornwell**, asking for a visual language that could hold both worlds. Her design captures that sense of being between places beautifully.

My thanks to **Draft2Digital**, whose quiet efficiency makes the practical side of independent publishing far easier to navigate.

I would also like to acknowledge: **Madame Flavour Teas** (www.madameflavour.com) and **Chilli Coffee Australia** (www.chillicoffee.com.au) whose teas and coffees have long been a source of inspiration for the flavours, aromas, and rituals that find their way into these pages. Their work reflects the same care and intention that sits at the heart of the Celestial Café.

And finally, thanks to you, dear reader. These stories were written to be lingered over—perhaps with a warm cup nearby—and it's a pleasure to share the Café with you.

ABOUT THE AUTHOR

Melody R. Green writes quiet, myth-touched fiction and reflective companion works where cafés become thresholds, magic is gentle, and transformation unfolds slowly.

Her stories are rooted in everyday rituals—tea, travel, conversation—and open into something more luminous. Through travelling tarot readers, angelic companions, and liminal places, Melody explores how change often arrives softly, through presence rather than force.

She is the author of ***Maggie McCready's Travelling Tarot Adventures*** and ***Larissa's Angelic Adventures***.

Alongside her fiction, Melody writes ***Notes from the Celestial Café***, a quiet monthly letter shared with a brew and a blessing, for readers who prefer reflection to urgency and depth to noise.

Originally from the UK and now living in Australia, she is rarely far from a good cup of tea or coffee, an over-imagined café menu, or a story waiting to be brewed.

Website: **www.melodyrgreenauthor.com**

Instagram: **www.instagram.com/melodyrgreenauthor**

Facebook: **www.facebook.com/melodyrgreenbooks**

Also By

MELODY R. GREEN

Maggie McCready's Travelling Tarot Adventures

BOOK 1: THE ANGEL TEA HOUSE

BOOK 2: THE PILGRIMS' WAY CAFE

BOOK 3: THE PENDRAGON TEAROOMS

MAGGIE McCREADY'S OMNIBUS

WISH BOMBS, BAKING SPELLS AND RECIPES

Larissa's Angelic Adventures

BOOK 1: CAFE ROMANTIQUE (Coming Soon)

Love Tales and Recipes

BOOK 1: A TIPSY MAN GOES NAKED

BOOK 2: NUTS ABOUT LOVE

Beloved, I Love You So

ALSO BY

MELODY R. GREEN

Maggie McCready's Travelling Tarot Adventures

THE ANGEL TEA HOUSE

BOOK 1

If you believe that some places hold more than they show, that a cup of tea can be a moment of grace, and that guidance often arrives quietly— The Angel Tea House was written for you.

Tucked away on Angel Street is a tea house where nothing is quite as ordinary as it seems. When Maggie McCready, a travelling tarot reader, steps inside, she finds herself drawn into a mystery where unseen forces stir and the cards speak with unexpected clarity. Here, intuition matters, kindness carries weight, and danger never announces itself loudly.

Written by a working tarot reader, this is cosy mystical fiction where magic is grounded, angels are attentive, and transformation begins with listening.

ALSO BY

MELODY R. GREEN

Maggie McCready's Travelling Tarot Adventures

THE PILGRIMS' WAY CAFE

BOOK 2

If you are drawn to ancient paths, sacred landscapes, and the quiet pull of places shaped by centuries of prayer and passage —The Pilgrims' Way Café was written for you.

Along Dartmoor's storied the Archangels' Way lies a café that serves more than food and shelter. When Maggie McCready arrives, she discovers a mystery woven into the land itself—one that calls for courage, discernment, and trust in the guidance of the tarot. As old spirits stir, Maggie must walk gently between worlds where the past still speaks.

Written by a working tarot reader, this is a story of sacred paths, unseen guardians, and magic that unfolds through care rather than confrontation.

ALSO BY

MELODY R. GREEN

Maggie McCready's Travelling Tarot Adventures

THE PENDRAGON TEAROOMS

BOOK 3

If you feel the pull of ancient kings, dragon power, and places where myth breathes beneath the everyday— The Pendragon Tea Rooms was written for you.

At the heart of Britain's most sacred sites stands a tea room where destiny gathers quietly. When Maggie McCready is drawn into its orbit, she must face both earthly and supernatural dangers, guided by the wisdom of the tarot and the fragile balance between light and shadow. Here, the lines between good and evil blur—and every choice carries weight.

Written by a working tarot reader, this is cosy mystical fiction rooted in Arthurian legend, quiet sovereignty, and the courage to serve without domination.

Also By

MELODY R. GREEN

Maggie McCready's Travelling Tarot Adventures

THE OMNIBUS

If you believe that some places hold more than they show, that tarot speaks most clearly when it is listened to with care, and that guidance often arrives quietly—this collection was written for you.

This omnibus brings together all three novels in The Maggie McCready Travelling Tarot Adventures, following Maggie McCready, a travelling tarot reader who offers insight over tea and a charmed biscuit—and finds herself drawn into mysteries where sacred places, unseen forces, and human lives quietly intertwine.

From a tea house on Angel Street, to an ancient pilgrims' path across Dartmoor, to the myth-laden heart of Britain itself, Maggie's journey unfolds through threshold places where hospitality is ritual, intuition is action, and power is exercised through listening rather than force. Each story deepens her relationships, her steadiness, and her spiritual authority—not through conquest, but through care.

Written by a working tarot reader, this is cosy mystical fiction where magic is grounded, danger is understated, and transformation unfolds slowly. Angels are attentive rather than spectacular, the land remembers what humans forget, and the smallest choices often carry the greatest weight.

ALSO BY

MELODY R. GREEN

Maggie McCready's Travelling Tarot Adventures

WISH BOMBS, BAKING SPELLS AND RECIPES

If you believe that intention matters, that the kitchen can be a sacred space, and that everyday acts of care can quietly change the world—this book was written for you.

Wish Bombs, Baking Spells and Recipes is an invitation to bring more light, warmth, and meaning into your life through simple, nourishing practices. Here, baking becomes ritual, stirring becomes prayer, and food is offered not for perfection, but for connection—with yourself, with others, and with something gently unseen.

This is not a spell book hidden behind complicated rules, nor a cookbook that demands performance. It is a companion for slow moments: recipes infused with intention, baking spells designed for real kitchens, and wish bombs created to hold hope, healing, and quiet joy. Everything inside is practical, accessible, and rooted in kindness rather than control.

Written by a working spiritual practitioner and creative, this book reflects lived practice—magic as something you do with your hands, your heart, and the ingredients already in your cupboard. Whether you are new to ritual or returning to it after time away, you are welcome here.

Awarded a 2025 Global Book Awards Bronze Medal, Wish Bombs, Baking Spells and Recipes is for readers who savour rather than rush, who believe that love is an ingredient, and who know that the smallest acts—offered with care—can ripple outward in beautiful ways.

This is magic you can share—and eat.

ALSO BY

MELODY R. GREEN

Love Tales and Recipes

A TIPSY MAN GOES NAKED

A collection of short stories where love, food, and memory intertwine.

A Tipsy Man Goes Naked is the first book in the Love Tales and Recipes series—a gathering of intimate stories that move across countries, centuries, and emotional landscapes. Each tale explores a different expression of love: tender, fleeting, reckless, enduring, sometimes joyful, sometimes bittersweet.

Food is never incidental in these stories. It carries memory, anchors relationships, and becomes a quiet language of its own. Alongside each piece of fiction is a recipe drawn from the world of the story—some simple, some indulgent—chosen not to instruct, but to deepen the experience.

Rather than a single narrative, this collection offers moments: fairy-tale echoes, grounded human encounters, and reflections on love as it is lived rather than idealised. The result is a book designed to be dipped into, shared, and returned to—perhaps with something warm on the stove.

A Tipsy Man Goes Naked is for readers who enjoy reflective short fiction, sensory storytelling, and the intimacy of stories told around a table.

ALSO BY

MELODY R. GREEN

Love Tales and Recipes

NUTS ABOUT LOVE

Stories of love told through seasons, cultures, and the rituals of the kitchen.

Nuts About Love continues the Love Tales and Recipes series with a collection shaped by the rhythm of the year. Moving from winter through to autumn, each story reflects a different emotional climate— grief and endurance, devotion and joy, inheritance and choice. Set across countries and cultures, these stories invite readers into kitchens, villages, and private moments where love reveals itself through care, patience, and shared nourishment. Alongside each tale is a recipe rooted in the setting of the story, offering a tangible connection to place and tradition.

Love here is not limited to romance. It appears as companionship, ancestry, resilience, and the quiet bonds that form over time. Some stories are gentle, others quietly devastating, but together they form a cohesive tapestry held together by seasonality, atmosphere, and a deep respect for everyday ritual.

Nuts About Love is a book to be read slowly and revisited— a collection that encourages pause, reflection, and the simple pleasure of sharing food and stories.

Coming Soon

MELODY R. GREEN

Larissa's Angelic Adventures

CAFE ROMANTIQUE

In this spin-off series to Maggie McCready's Travelling Tarot Adventures, Maggie has ascended to become an angel, and must learn the nuances of her new role as an angelic helper to humans.

Larissa takes up the celestial mantle and embarks on her first mission in the evocative French town of Carcassonne. Here, Larissa must help Marguerite, a determined baker at the Café Romantique, overcome the persistent obstacles posed by a scheming mayor whose true motives are shrouded in secrets from the distant past.

As unravelled memories of the Albigensian Crusade and the Cathars come to light, Larissa's wisdom and compassion empower Marguerite to transform from victim to victor, exposing greed and restoring justice.

This captivating blend of mysticism, history, and hope promises readers a journey that bridges worlds, challenges the boundaries between good and evil, and celebrates the courage found in truth and self-discovery.

This series is perfect for fans of cozy mysteries, light fantasy, and stories featuring strong, relatable female protagonists.

ALSO FROM

MELODY R. GREEN

Notes from the Celestial Cafe

Notes from the Celestial Cafe is a quiet monthly letter, written from the space between worlds. Each note is shared with a suggested brew and a small blessing, and is intended to be read slowly—without urgency, instruction or expectation.

Find out more here: info@melodyrgreenauthor.com

www.ingramcontent.com/pod-product-compliance
Lightning Source LLC
LaVergne TN
LVHW050609100826
845148LV00015B/3186

* 9 7 8 1 7 6 4 1 8 8 9 2 0 *